Special thanks to my biggest fan, Nira, my wonderful mother, Doris, my sister, Laurie, and my Englewood Library co-workers, Donna-Lynne, Amy, and Susan for their unfailing support.

To my loving brother, Donny, who, like Sammy, has finally found a new home.

-Marguerite Sansone

Dear Wesson,

Enjoy Sammy!

Best,

M. Sansone

PRT0114B

Printed in the United States

ISBN-13: 9781620861882
ISBN-10: 1620861887

www.mascotbooks.com

Sammy and the Wrecking Ball

Marguerite Sansone

Illustrated by Joe Bevill

Sammy the snake was a slip sliding soul
Who whistled a tune with each wiggle and roll.
One sunshiny day he slipped into his den,
A cozy wood shack in a warm, grassy glen.

A bang and a crash! Sammy peeked through the pane,
Then hissed when he spotted a ball on a chain.
It teetered and tottered about in the air,
Then headed straight over to Sammy's back stair.

"Oh no!" Sammy cried. "Won't you please stop this minute?
You'll wreck my poor shack and the precious things in it."
He made for the trees with his suitcase in tow,
While his snug little house suffered blow after blow.

"Now what," Sammy moaned, "can a little snake do?
I've nowhere to go and no house to tend to."
He lowered his head and then rattled his tail,
Passed the steep rocky slope to the wide dusty trail.

The wreckage and grit from his crumbled-down shack
Filled the air as the yellow crane followed his track.
The ball hovered above him, then plunged to the ground.
Sammy quaked in his scales without making a sound.

Soon the dust from the site made the ball disappear.
Sammy lost complete sight of that menacing sphere.
He flicked out his tongue and attempted to flee,
Wriggled over bent cans and bumped into a tree.

He crawled up a rock nestled off to the side,
Squirmed around and about it to see where to hide.

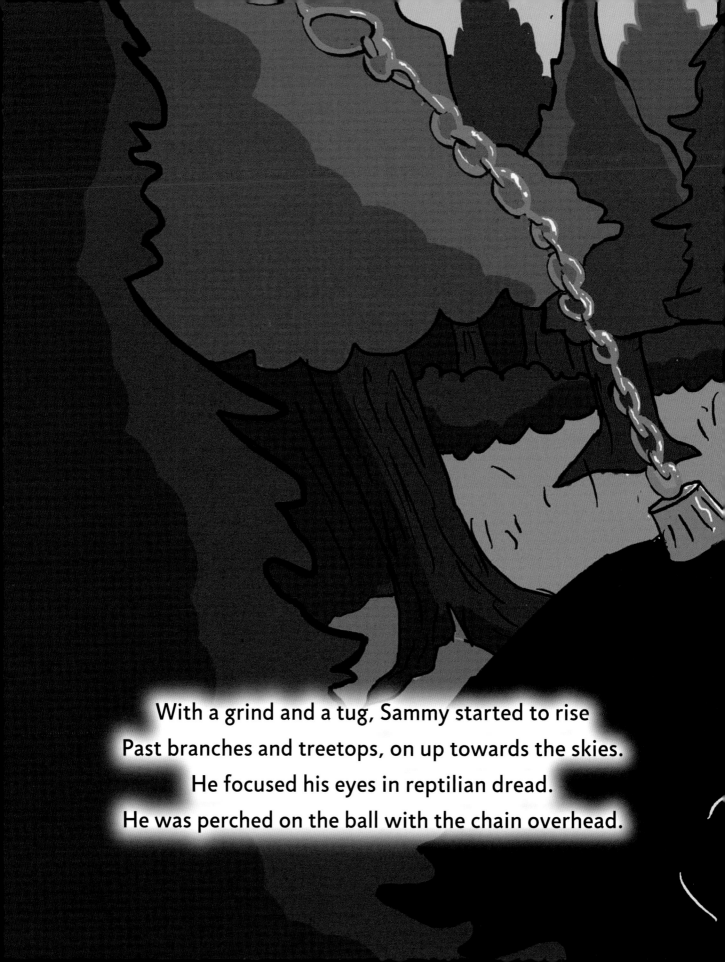

With a grind and a tug, Sammy started to rise
Past branches and treetops, on up towards the skies.
He focused his eyes in reptilian dread.
He was perched on the ball with the chain overhead.

"Oh no!" Sammy cried. "I must leave this place now!"
He spotted a plant hanging from a tree bough.
He reached out his tail and clutched onto the vine,
Then flew off the ball with a hiss and a whine.

He swung over valleys, green fields full of crop,
Till his tail lost its grip and he started to drop.

Sammy noticed some broken-up logs in a pile,
Then dragged his tail over and rested awhile.

He gazed at the woodpile all splintered from wear,
And thought it could use just a little repair.

He touched up the holes with some slushy creek silt,
On the roof of the house he so lovingly built.
I am safe, Sammy thought, as he slithered in style,
Far away from that ball in my sturdy log pile.

He carved out a sign which he stuck in the grass,
"Sammy's Nature Reserve, Cranes forbidden to pass."
Sammy whistled a tune with a wiggle and roll,
For once again, he was a slip sliding soul.

About the Author

Marguerite Sansone is a Paraprofessional Children's Librarian who loves to write stories for children in verse. She escapes to the country on weekends where she comes in contact with all sorts of crawling critters, including snakes. Needless to say, Ms. Sansone prefers to write about snakes rather than encounter them in person. Ms. Sansone is currently working on a mystery novel.

Have a book idea?

Contact us at:

Mascot Books
560 Herndon Parkway
Suite 120
Herndon, VA 20170

info@mascotbooks.com | www.mascotbooks.com